"Well, it has to be in here somewhere," Ms. Moriarty said when Zach told her his ball was missing.

Only it wasn't.

Every boy and girl searched the room, and even the bathroom. They looked in the closet and in every single cubby. They looked under Ms. Moriarty's desk and under their own desks. No one could find the Will Hanley ball. It was like they were having their own private scavenger hunt, searching for one item in particular: Zach's ball.

But it was gone.

ALSO BY #1 BESTSELLER MIKE LUPICA

PUFFIN BOOKS
An imprint of Penguin Random House LLC
375 Hudson Street
New York, NY 10014

Published simultaneously in the United States of America by Philomel Books and Puffin Books,
imprints of Penguin Random House LLC, 2018

LIBRARY OF CONGRESS CATALOGING-IN-PUBLICATION DATA IS AVAILABLE.
Puffin Books ISBN: 9780425289372

Printed in the United States of America

1 3 5 7 9 10 8 6 4 2

Design by Maria Fazio
Text set in Fournier MT Std

THE ZACH & ZOE MYSTERIES
THE MISSING BASEBALL

Mike Lupica

illustrated by

Chris Danger

Puffin Books

This book is for the real Zach, who always played big, in everything.

ONE

"It's just a baseball," Zoe Walker said to her brother, Zach. "You have lots of signed baseballs."

Zach and Zoe Walker were eight, and they were twins. They didn't look exactly alike, but they did think a lot alike. They just didn't always think exactly alike.

Like right now, for instance. They were eating breakfast at the kitchen table before school.

Zach knew his sister was both right and wrong. He did have a lot of signed baseballs, that much was true. Some were gifts from his parents. Some he had gotten signed by professional baseball players. Zach and Zoe's father, Danny, worked as a sports reporter on TV. Often, he would take Zach and Zoe to special events where they got to meet the players face-to-face.

But the ball they were talking about now was different from the others. Zach loved that ball more than the rest, and he was sure Zoe knew it.

The twins loved competing against each other in almost everything. In fact, Zoe even made talking a competition. She seemed to be doing it now.

"It's not just another ball," Zach said. "You know it's the ball Will Hanley hit for a home run—the ball *I* caught!"

It had happened a couple of weeks before. Their parents took Zach and Zoe to a game at Fenway Park. Zach's favorite player, Will

Hanley, was playing. His team only visited Boston once each season. The family all sat in the Monster Seats at Fenway. The Monster Seats are on top of the famous wall in left field called the Green Monster. Looking down at the field from their seats, Zach couldn't believe how small everything looked. It was almost as if they were watching a game in their backyard.

"I know Will Hanley is your favorite baseball player," Zoe said. "And I know why. He's smaller than just about everybody in Major League Baseball. But he plays big, same as you."

"And he's a second baseman, same as me," Zach added, as he spooned cereal into his mouth.

"But even though he's your favorite player, and even though you caught that home run ball," Zoe said, "it's still just a ball."

She smiled to herself, like she'd just won the argument. Zach glanced over at their mom, who was grinning from across the kitchen.

She pointed to her watch, which meant it was almost time to walk to the corner to catch their school bus.

"You know what I always tell you," their mom said. "It's not the souvenirs that matter. It's the memories that go with them."

"But that's the thing," Zach said. "This ball is part of my memory."

The twins' dad, Danny Walker, had been a star basketball player. He started playing when he was Zach and Zoe's age. Then he went on to play in high school and college. He even played a few years in the NBA. But he hurt his knee and had to retire early. He was the smallest player in every game he ever played in his life. Zach and Zoe were also small for their age, and Danny always made sure to tell them size is important. Just not in the way they thought. It's how big you play that really matters.

Now he worked as a sports reporter on TV. Their mom said he was just as good at doing that as he'd been at everything else in his life.

When he bought the family tickets in the Monster Seats, he'd had no idea it would turn into a monster day for Zach. In the first inning, Will Hanley hit the ball so far and so high, it cleared the top of the wall and ended up in Zach's glove. Everyone in their section cheered.

After the game, Zach and his dad waited in the parking lot with a crowd of other fans. That's where Will Hanley and the players on the visiting team would board their bus. Zach knew his dad had special connections as a TV reporter. He could get them into the clubhouse if he wanted. But Zach also knew his dad didn't think it was right for reporters to ask for autographs, even if the autograph was for one of their kids.

"If you want Will Hanley's autograph, you'll have to wait like everyone else," Danny said to Zach after the game.

For as long as Zach and Zoe could remember, their dad had taught them to always do the right thing, whether it had to do with sports or anything else in their lives. Even if all they wanted was to get a baseball signed by their favorite player, they had to do it the fair way.

So Zach waited with the other kids on the street that ran along the first-base side of Fenway Park. Slowly, he and his dad worked their way to the front of the crowd, happy that the much bigger crowd was waiting up the block where the Red Sox players parked their cars.

Finally, Will Hanley walked out of the park wearing his normal clothes. Somehow he looked even smaller than he did in his baseball uniform.

"Mr. Hanley!" Zach shouted. "Over here! Please."

(His mom would say later that everything worked out because Zach had been nice. She always said you can never go wrong being nice.)

Will Hanley stopped to see where the voice

had come from. When he looked over, he saw
Zach holding out his home run ball.

"Mr. Hanley," Zach said, "this is the ball
you hit over the Green Monster in the first
inning."

Will smiled at him.

"If I asked for it back, would you give it to
me?" he asked.

"Yes, sir," Zach said, without hesitation.

"Well, how about I just sign it for you,"
he said. "I never hit a ball over that old green
wall before. So I already know I'll never forget
today. Now neither of us will."

Zach handed him the ball and the Sharpie his dad had given him. Will Hanley signed the ball, handed it back, shook Zach's hand, and then walked up the steps and onto the bus.

That ball now sat in Zach's backpack. He was bringing it to their third-grade classroom for a very special show-and-tell. Half the kids in the class would be presenting today, and the other half on Thursday. All the kids in the class had been asked to bring something important to them. They were even encouraged to wear a T-shirt of their favorite player or team if they had one. This was just one part of the school's annual Spirit Week. If you weren't a sports fan, you could wear a T-shirt of your favorite TV show or book or band or movie.

Zach wore his No. 19 Hanley shirt. Zoe, who loved books as much as she did sports (maybe even more), wore the Harry Potter T-shirt their parents bought her when they'd visited the Wizarding World of Harry Potter™ in Florida over spring break. Zoe had already finished the first three Harry Potter books and was on to the fourth, even though she was only eight. She was even bringing her favorite Harry Potter book, the first one, with her to school today.

"That's your thing of value?" Zach said to her as they grabbed their backpacks. "Seriously?"

Zoe smiled. "A really good story is as valuable as anything. Right, Mom?"

"A hundred percent," Tess Walker said. "Now both of you get going or the story this morning will be that you missed the bus."

None of them knew at the time that the biggest story of Spirit Week was just beginning for Zach and Zoe Walker, and that it was going to be the best kind:

A mystery.

About an autographed baseball that turned out to be anything but just another ball.

TWO

The kids looked forward to Spirit Week every year. Five straight days of fun activities, friendly competition, and wearing silly outfits to school.

The teachers divided each grade into two teams, the Blue team and the White team. Then they added up the points for each competition to decide the champion at the end of the week. There were two third-grade classes at Middletown Elementary, but instead of just having the classes play against each other, they mixed up the kids to make it more fun.

The winning team didn't just win bragging rights, they also won a pizza party at Joe's Pizzeria, the best pizza shop in town.

Already, they'd had an epic tug-of-war, a capture the flag game, and a talent competition modeled after the TV show *America's Got Talent*. There was still a soccer match to be played, relay races to run, and an all-school scavenger hunt.

Last year, the championship came down to the big baseball game played on the last day of Spirit Week. Zach's team won the game and the pizza party. This year, for fun, the other kids had voted to make Zach the captain of the Blue team and Zoe the captain of the White.

"Your team's not beating mine two years in a row," Zoe said as they got off the bus at school Wednesday morning.

"We're already ahead now that we won the tug-of-war," Zach said.

"Barely," Zoe said.

"You know what Dad says, little sister," Zach said. "This isn't like horseshoes. They don't give you points for coming close."

He sometimes called her "little sister" because he was born exactly one minute before she was. Lately, when he did that, Zoe would point out that she was a half-inch taller, and say, "You might be older, but I'm bigger."

But today she just ignored it and said, "You know it's going to come down to the baseball game again."

"Can't wait," Zach said.

Zach loved any kind of big championship game, whether it was baseball or soccer or basketball. But he loved baseball the most. It was another reason he couldn't wait for the game on Friday. Their dad, who had played in many big games, always told Zach and Zoe the same thing, no matter what sport they happened to be playing at the time: you had to value every one of these games, because you never knew how many of them you'd get to play in your life.

For now, Zach was most interested in showing off his Will Hanley ball to his classmates. There were twenty kids in their classroom, with desks in the middle and cubbies on the side. There were posters on the walls and a view from the windows of the fields below them. Behind their teacher Ms. Moriarty's desk was a whiteboard with some markers at the bottom. Zach and Zoe agreed there was just something about this room that made them feel happy, like something good and exciting was going to happen there every single day. Their mom always told them it was part of the adventure of learning, the greatest adventure of all.

Today, though, Zach felt like he was a teacher, too. Standing at the front of the classroom, he explained to his classmates why his ball was important to him. "Catching it the way I did made me feel, just for one moment, like I was in the game myself."

He wished Zoe could have done the talking for him. She loved speaking in front of their class. She always had her hand up when Ms. Moriarty asked a question. It didn't matter which subject. If Zoe had to discuss a reading assignment, she always seemed to pick up on things that Zach had missed, almost as if she'd gone through the whole book looking for clues.

"Zoe sees things other people don't," their mom liked to say.

"Wait, does that mean I don't?" Zach had asked her one time.

His mom had smiled at him. "You see things like your dad. For instance, you can spot somebody open in a basketball or soccer game before anyone else. You can see something on the baseball field before it happens. Zoe looks at the world like it's a puzzle she's trying to solve."

When they'd gotten to school, Zach had been surprised to see he wasn't the only one in class wearing a Will Hanley shirt. So was Mateo Salazar, who'd only moved to Middletown and joined their class a month ago. When Zach got up for show-and-tell, holding his baseball in his hand, he noticed Mateo staring at the ball as if it were made of solid gold.

Zach finished his presentation with something he'd heard his dad say a lot. "Mr. Hanley

shows that size really does matter in sports," Zach said. "The size of your talent and the size of your heart."

Then he went over and placed the ball on the windowsill next to two other signed baseballs kids had brought to class that day. Ms. Moriarty wanted them away from their desks, so no one would stare at them all morning instead of paying attention to the other speakers.

But it wasn't just sports items on display. One girl brought the best coin from her coin collection. One boy, Malik Jones, brought a chair he and his dad built together. Ms. Moriarty brought her cat, Sundance, who spent most of the morning pushing a ball of yarn around on her desk. Ms. Moriarty promised to bring Sundance to class on both days of show-and-tell, to be fair to all the students.

Zoe had her Harry Potter book. When she finished her presentation to the class, it was time to go to lunch. Everybody was headed out of the room and down the hall toward the cafeteria when Mateo said he'd forgotten his lunch in his cubby.

Zach watched as Mateo ran back toward the classroom. Zach didn't know Mateo very well yet, mostly because Mateo was a shy boy who had kept to himself since coming to Middletown Elementary. But Zach liked the fact that they were both huge fans of Will Hanley.

When Mateo returned, out of breath, Zach asked, "You get what you needed?"

"Oh, yeah," Mateo said.

They all went to lunch. When they got back to the room, Zach noticed that all the baseballs were where they'd been left.

All except one.

Zach's ball was gone.

THREE

"Well, it has to be in here somewhere," Ms. Moriarty said when Zach told her his ball was missing.

Only it wasn't.

Every boy and girl searched the room, and even the bathroom. They looked in the closet and in every single cubby. They looked under Ms. Moriarty's desk and under their own desks. No one could find the Will Hanley ball. It was like they were having their own private

scavenger hunt, searching for one item in particular: Zach's ball.

But it was gone.

Zach didn't want the other kids in the class to see how upset he was. But he just couldn't help himself. His mom would remind him that the memory is more important than the ball itself. But this was different. Will Hanley was his favorite player. Zach didn't know when he'd get the chance to see him play again. And he sure didn't think he was ever going to catch another home run ball that Will hit, at Fenway Park or anywhere else.

This really, really wasn't just another baseball. Not to him.

"What if somebody picked it up by mistake?" Malik wondered aloud.

"You mean somebody came into our classroom, picked the ball up off the windowsill, and forgot to put it back?" Zoe said.

"But no one else besides Ms. Moriarty was in our classroom while we were at lunch," said Zach.

One of the other girls, Lily Holmes, who Zach and Zoe thought talked a little too much about other kids, pointed out that Mateo had briefly come back to the classroom alone while everybody else was on their way to lunch.

"And he does seem to be a big fan of Will Hanley," Lily said, pointing at Mateo's shirt, which looked exactly the same as the one Zach was wearing.

"I would never do something like that," Mateo said. "I heard Zach say how much that ball means to him. I would never steal it! I've never stolen anything in my life!"

"Nobody's accusing you of stealing," Ms. Moriarty said.

"All I did was come back for my lunch," Mateo said. "I didn't even go near the windows."

He was looking straight at Zach, almost like he was begging Zach to believe him.

"Mateo," Zach said, "I'm not accusing you of anything. I just want my ball back. I'm sorry I even brought it with me to school today."

"Where could it have gone?" Malik said.

"That's the mystery," Zoe said.

Zoe had noticed when they got back to their classroom that two of the four windows were now open.

"These windows weren't open when we left the room for lunch," Zoe observed.

"It's such a nice day out that I wanted to let some breeze in," Ms. Moriarty said. "So I opened all the windows. But then a gust of wind blew in and scattered the papers on my desk all over the floor. I decided it would be safer just to open a couple of windows."

"But before you closed them, is it possible one of the balls might have rolled off the windowsill without you noticing?" Zoe asked.

"I guess it's possible," Ms. Moriarty said. "But I doubt the breeze was big enough to blow a baseball around the way it did my papers."

"Whatever happened," Zach said, "there were three baseballs here before, and now there are only two."

His ball had either disappeared on its own, which he knew wasn't possible, or now belonged to somebody else.

He wished Ms. Moriarty's cat, Sundance, could talk. The cat was the only one who'd been here the whole time.

FOUR

When it was time for the bus home, Zach couldn't find Zoe. He started to think maybe she had left something back in their classroom. But about two minutes before their bus was scheduled to leave, she came running up to him and they boarded the bus together. She was out of breath, but had a big smile on her face.

"Where have you been?" he asked, worried.

"Investigating," she said, like it was obvious. "Did you find my ball?"

She shook her head. "Sorry."

"But you found something, didn't you?" Zach said. After all, she wasn't smiling for nothing.

"Maybe," she said.

Zach sighed. "I can always tell when you think you know something no one else does."

One time, Zach told her he didn't think her favorite sport was soccer or softball or even basketball. It was solving mysteries.

"I don't know something," she said. "But I did find something."

She unzipped the front pocket of her backpack and showed him a key. It was round at the top, almost like a coin.

Zach gazed at the key for a long while. "What do you think it means?" he asked.

"It means we have our first clue," said Zoe.

FIVE

On the bus ride home, Zach and Zoe went over what they knew so far about the missing baseball. They were always bouncing ideas off each other. At home, in school, and everywhere in between.

They knew it was nearly impossible to solve the mystery in one afternoon. But they couldn't help but wonder if they might have missed something.

"I don't think Mateo took it," Zach said.

"He could have," his sister said, "whether we want to admit it or not."

"But he really was only in the classroom for a few seconds. And even if he did take the ball—which I don't think he did—where would he stash it?" Zach said.

Zoe thought for a minute. "And we looked in everyone's cubby, including his."

Zach shook his head and sighed. "I'm going to keep looking until we solve this puzzle and find my ball," he said.

"Same," Zoe said, without missing a beat.

They agreed to tell Mr. Parker, the school's maintenance man and custodian, to be on the lookout for Zach's ball. But they would have to wait until Friday. Mr. Parker had gone away for a few days to attend his nephew's college graduation. He'd left right after classes ended. Though Zach was anxious to ask Mr. Parker about the ball, he also hoped Mr. Parker would be back in time to coach the big Spirit Week baseball game Friday afternoon.

Zach couldn't help it, though. He was still upset about his missing ball. But somehow, the challenge of trying to find it made him feel better. So he tried to focus on that instead.

Later that night, while eating dinner with their parents, Zoe explained how she'd found the key. "After school, I asked Ms. Moriarty if she could help me look for clues outside the windows of the classroom, in case the ball had fallen down there without her noticing. I just wanted to make sure I hadn't missed anything," Zoe said.

"That sounds like something you would do," their mom said.

"You know what we like to say, Mom," Zach said. "That's just Zoe being Zoe."

"So we poked around in the bushes," Zoe said, "even though it was muddy from all the rain we had yesterday."

"But no baseball . . ." their dad stated.

Zoe shook her head. "Nope. Just the key." She held it up for everyone to see.

"The good news," Zach said, "is that Zoe's sure it's a clue."

"The bad news," Zoe cut in, "is that it's not the kind of key that fits the locks on any of the classroom cabinets. I know because we tried the key on a few locks before it was time to get on the bus. And it's too short to be the key for a door. But Ms. Moriarty told me to hold on to it so we could do more investigating tomorrow if we got the chance."

"What if it's just some old key that's been lying out there for a long time?" their dad asked.

"Dad, the ball had to have fallen out the window. Even though I can't prove it did," Zoe said. "If it didn't, it means somebody really might have stolen it. I don't believe anybody in our class would do that."

"What if the person who found the ball dropped the key at the same time?" their mom wondered aloud.

"But then why wouldn't that person just return the ball?" Zach pointed out.

Zoe grinned at her brother. "Maybe that person thought it was just another ball."

"But it's a signed ball," Zach said. "And pretty new. And it has 'Major League Baseball' written on it."

"I'm still working on a theory about that," Zoe said.

Their mom agreed with Zoe that the key had to be a clue. If they could only find the owner of the key, it might help them solve the mystery.

"There's got to be an explanation for where the ball is," Zoe said.

"So then where is it?" Zach said.

"Don't know," his sister said. Then, pointing at him with the key, she added, "Yet."

SIX

While they were loading the dishwasher after dinner that night (one of their weekly chores), Zach asked Zoe if she loved sports as much as he did.

"Doesn't matter," she said. "All that matters is that I love sports as much as *I* do."

"But what do you love most about sports?" Zach asked her, curious.

"Like Dad always says," Zoe replied. "Playing helps you be the best you can be. Almost like you're competing against yourself."

"Okay, so how'd you like to compete against me right now in a game of one-on-one basketball?"

Zoe didn't hesitate. "It's on," she said. And with that, they raced out the front door.

Zach and Zoe loved the basket their dad had hung in their driveway, adjusted to the perfect height for them. He told them it was the same type of basket he'd had in his driveway when he was growing up in Middletown.

"It was the first real basketball classroom I'd ever had," he said. "It was where I practiced dribbling and worked on my moves. I'd even set up chairs to act as imaginary teammates and throw passes at them."

Sometimes Zach and Zoe would bring out chairs and do the same thing. But tonight they didn't need any imaginary players. They had each other.

Zach and Zoe still struggled a little bit to get their shots up to an eight-foot basket, which was two feet lower than a standard basketball hoop. But the more they played, the better they got at shooting and the higher they were able to jump. Plus, they were both fast, good dribblers, and difficult to guard. Sometimes when they played in the driveway, Zach felt as if he were playing against himself. Playing with Zoe was like looking into a mirror. He knew that while he was getting the best out of himself, he was getting the best out of his sister, too.

They were playing their usual game—the first to reach seven baskets wins. Even though sometimes players had to win by two baskets, they agreed that for tonight, it would only have to be one. Zach quickly got ahead 4–2. But Zoe, never one to give up easily, came right back to tie him. Then she pulled ahead 6–5 on a jump shot she banked in off the backboard. But Zach knocked the ball away from her, picked it up, and made the outside shot that tied the game at 6–6.

They were playing winners' outs. That meant if you scored, you kept the ball.

It was still Zach's ball.

"Just so you know," Zoe said, "I know what you're going to do."

"Tell me, if you're so smart," he said.

"Nope," Zoe said. "That would give you the edge." She pointed to her head. "Up here, I still have the edge."

"But you may have noticed that I have the ball," Zach said, shifting the ball from one hand to the other.

Zoe laughed. "For now."

Against most other players, it was Zach's brain that gave him the edge. But that wasn't the case with his sister. Sometimes it really did feel like she was thinking right along with him. Like she had this way of getting inside his brain anytime she wanted to.

But for once, he was one step ahead of her. Zach had a good idea what Zoe thought he was going to do—the crossover move, which was the first their dad had taught them. It was one of Zach's favorite moves. With a crossover, you quickly switched the ball from one hand to the other while dribbling. It was a way of faking out your opponent. Zach had used the move plenty of times to drive right past Zoe in games like this one. She had done the same against him.

Tonight, though, he was going to use a double crossover, a move he'd been working on when Zoe wasn't around. He planned to go from his right hand to his left and then back to his right.

And that's exactly what he did. As soon as he dribbled the ball with his left hand, Zoe, who was expecting a normal crossover, jumped to her right to cut him off. Just as Zach had planned. When she did, Zach went back to his right hand. It gave him the opening he needed to drive past her for the layup that made the final score 7–6.

As soon as the ball came bouncing down onto the driveway, Zoe's right hand shot up. Zach took a step toward her and put up his hand to mirror hers. It looked as if they were about to give each other a high five. And they were. But first, they spun completely around, bumped elbows and hips, and then came the leaping high five. Their mom said it was like a combination of a secret handshake and a touch-down dance in football. They always did it no matter who won the game.

"You out-thought me!" Zoe exclaimed.

"Wow!" Zach said. "That's even better than winning the game."

He tossed his sister the ball, and she went to put it back in the small equipment shed next to the garage. Inside the shed, there were basketballs and soccer balls, baseballs and bats, and floats for the pool in their backyard. There was even room for their tennis rackets. Their mom liked to call it the Walker family sporting goods store.

Zoe put the basketball in the bin with the other balls and closed the door to the shed.

But as she turned the key sticking out of the lock, one she'd never paid much attention to before, she noticed it looked a lot like the one she'd found outside their classroom window.

"Does this look familiar?" she said to Zach, showing him the key.

"It doesn't just look familiar," Zach said. "It looks like it might be another clue."

Zoe smiled. "Even better."

SEVEN

There were more Spirit Week events the next day at school. They started with relay races in the morning, followed by a scavenger hunt that took them all over the school grounds looking for objects their teachers had hidden. The soccer game for their class was scheduled for the afternoon.

Zoe told Zach she wasn't nearly as interested in the school scavenger hunt as she was in her own.

"I'm still on a mission to find your ball," she said to her brother.

"*We're* on a mission," Zach said.

Ms. Moriarty and Mr. Jerome, the teacher of the other third-grade class, led them all around the school, hunting for items on the checklist all the kids carried with them: a pack of baseball cards, a comic book, a Frisbee, a can of tennis balls, one of Ms. Moriarty's Taylor Swift CDs, and a shiny silver dollar that Mr. Jerome had brought. Each grade had their own list of items to search for.

But even as both Blue and White teams looked for objects, sending up cheers when somebody found one of the items, Zach and Zoe kept their eyes open for clues about the Will Hanley ball.

They made it all the way down to the field where the big Spirit Week baseball game would be played the next day. Then Zoe stopped cold in her tracks. Zach saw her staring at the equipment shed where Mr. Parker kept the school's bats and balls. It was next to the machine he used to make the chalk lines on the field look as white as possible.

"You're staring at that shed like it's one of the items we're supposed to be looking for," Zach said to his sister.

"It's not that," Zoe said. "I'm just thinking that Mr. Parker's shed looks a lot like the one we have at home. Just a bigger version."

She ran over to where Ms. Moriarty was watching students look through the bushes near the baseball field.

"Ms. Moriarty?" Zoe began. "Do you think I could check and see if the key I found yesterday unlocks the equipment shed?" If the key she'd found outside their classroom window fit the lock for the shed, they might be one step closer to finding Zach's ball.

"I promise you, Zoe," Ms. Moriarty said. "Mr. Jerome and I didn't hide any of the items for the scavenger hunt inside that shed."

"I didn't think so," Zoe said. "But the key I found looks a lot like the one we use on the lock for our shed at home. And what if it opens the door to the shed, and I find Zach's ball inside?"

She could feel her heart beating so hard, it was as if it were trying to jump right out of her chest.

"No reason not to give it a try," Ms. Moriarty said.

She called over and asked Mr. Jerome to stay with the other third-graders, who had now moved their search to the soccer field. Ms. Moriarty, Zach and Zoe walked over to the shed together. Zoe held the key in her hand, put the key in the lock, turned it slightly, and . . . it opened!

"It works!" she said.

Ms. Moriarty pulled the shed doors open.

Zoe looked around inside. She saw bats leaning against one wall, an old baseball mitt, some extra bases, and all the equipment Mr. Parker used to take care of the field.

In the corner was a big canvas bag with balls inside.

"Can I dump out the balls?" Zoe asked Ms. Moriarty.

"I don't see why not," Ms. Moriarty responded.

"You're going to be right, I just know it," Zach said to his sister, feeling her excitement now.

"This really is going to be the end of our own scavenger hunt!" Zoe bounced on the balls of her feet.

Zoe grabbed the bag and turned it upside down. A bunch of dirty baseballs rolled out. Some of them looked older than the shed itself. They quickly went through them one by one, knowing they couldn't spend all day in here. They had a scavenger hunt to get back to.

But not one ball was Zach's.

Zach and Zoe looked at each other, the same disappointment on both their faces.

"I was so sure we were going to find it," Zoe said.

Zach shrugged at his sister and smiled, not wanting her to feel worse than she already did.

"So we keep looking," he said. "You're not giving up, are you?"

"Never," Zoe said.

"Why don't you hold on to that key, Zoe," Ms. Moriarty said. "In case it leads to another clue."

They came back to the classroom for the rest of show-and-tell before heading to lunch. Sundance, Ms. Moriarty's cat, was playing with a ball of yarn on the teacher's desk. At one point, he pushed it off the desk and onto the floor.

Zoe picked up the yarn and put it back on the desk, smiling at the cat as she did.

"Thank you," she said.

Zach said, "I didn't do anything."

"I was talking to Sundance," she said.

"What does that mean?"

"I'll tell you later," Zoe said, and they went to lunch.

EIGHT

Once they finished lunch, the only ball Zach and Zoe worried about was the one being used in the Blue vs. White soccer game that afternoon.

Zach's team, the Blue team, jumped out to a 2–0 lead. But Zoe's team came right back to tie. Zoe scored the White team's second goal on a sweet play, splitting two defenders and pushing the ball past Malik, the Blue team's goalie.

Finally, the score was tied 4–4, with two minutes left in the game. They were all having so much fun running up and down the field. This had become a school day no one wanted to end. It was how Zach and Zoe felt whenever they played in the yard after dinner. All they wanted was to keep running around, even as they ran out of daylight.

Zach once told Zoe that sports sometimes made him feel happy and sad at the same time. Happy to play, but sad when the game had to come to an end.

After some time, Ms. Moriarty looked at her watch and gave them the one minute warning. The score was still 4–4. The fourth graders had finished their own races on another field and come over to watch. So the cheers were even louder than they'd been the whole game.

Zach thought of something his mom liked to say: this was more fun than fun.

Zach was playing center midfielder. It was the same position he played on his travel team in the fall. He loved being a center middie because he always found himself right in the middle of the action. Sometimes he'd even go from defense to offense on the same play.

He was definitely in the middle of the action now, moving past midfield with the ball. His teammate Mateo was on his right. Zach had some open field in front of him. They both did. He began picking up speed, pushing the ball with his right foot, then his left.

He felt like he was flying.

In moments like this, his mom said he turned himself into a streak of light.

He gave a quick fake to his left and moved past Lily, who was playing defense for the White team. Then Zach spotted Mateo in the corner of his eye. He knew by now that Mateo wasn't really very good at soccer, or very fast. Though no one in the game was trying harder than he was.

So Zach slowed down just enough to let Mateo catch up with him. They were closing in on the White team's goalkeeper, Kari Stuart. Everyone knew she was the best goalie their age in town.

The only defender between them was Alex Rather, one of Zach's teammates in travel soccer. Zach and Alex had been playing soccer together since first grade. After all that time, Alex knew Zach's moves inside and out. And he knew Zach loved making a good pass just as much as he loved scoring himself.

So Alex moved just a little bit in Mateo's direction, ready to cut off a pass. It was almost like he was daring Zach to take the shot himself.

In the very next moment, Zach put on one more burst of speed. He angled to his left as if he were going to shoot the ball and try to win the game.

But Zach wanted Mateo to score the game-winning goal.

He could take the shot himself, but Zach knew how great it would be for the new kid to score instead. Maybe it would even help Mateo forget that some kids had accused him of taking Zach's ball. Though they hadn't thought that for very long.

Zach made sure to keep his eyes on Kari the whole time. But that was just another fake. As soon as Mateo was wide open, Zach pushed the ball over to him with his right foot. Mateo didn't hesitate or break stride. Kari was out of position because Zach's fake had convinced her he was going to shoot. Mateo had so much wide-open net, he couldn't miss. He kicked the ball and . . .

GOAL!

Blue team 5, White team 4.

Everyone on the Blue team ran toward Mateo, cheering. But Mateo ran straight for Zach as soon as the ball was in the goal.

"You didn't have to pass me the ball," he said. "You could have scored the goal yourself."

Zach shook his head. "Nope," he said. "I had to pass it to you."

"Why?" Mateo asked.

"For the best reason in the world," Zach said. "It was the right play."

They jumped into each other and bumped chests.

NINE

At dinner on Thursday night, Zach and Zoe updated their parents on the Spirit Week scores. The Blue team had five points, and so did the White. All that was left was the baseball game on Friday afternoon.

The winner of the game would win Spirit Week for the third grade this year.

But the number one thing on Zach and Zoe's mind was still the missing Will Hanley baseball.

"I was positive we were going to find it in Mr. Parker's shed," Zach said.

Zoe turned to her brother. "What if we don't find it at all. How sad will you be?"

"Very," Zach said. "Not gonna lie. Think about it: what are the odds I'll ever catch another home run ball hit by my favorite baseball player?"

"But you'll still have the memory of that ball ending up in the pocket of your glove," his dad said. "No one can take that away from you."

"But I want both, Dad," Zach said. "The ball and the memory. Does that make sense?"

"Perfect sense," his dad said.

"Just don't ever forget how hard your sister looked for a ball that didn't even belong to her," their mom said.

"Still looking," Zoe reminded her mom. "I'm not giving up."

"That attitude kind of runs in this family," Tess said.

After they helped clear the table, Zach and Zoe decided to go for one of their evening walks. It was the time of day when Zach and Zoe did their best talking, and their best thinking. They were only allowed to walk to the corner and back, so their mom could watch them as she sat on the front porch. But it didn't matter how far they went. Just walking together would stir up some of their best ideas.

"That ball is still at school somewhere, I just know it," Zoe said, as they started off down the block.

"If it is, you'll find it," Zach assured her.

Zoe gave him a gentle poke with her elbow. "And if I find it . . . I mean, *when* I find it . . . can I keep it? Sort of like a reward?"

"Absolutely, totally, one hundred percent . . . no!" he said.

They laughed.

"But when I do find it, it's going to feel like winning a trophy," Zoe said.

"One you'll have earned," Zach added.

They bumped fists and turned for home. Halfway to their house, Zoe challenged Zach to race the rest of the way. It was like she was bringing Spirit Week home by adding one last competition to the day.

They took off running, and in that moment, there were two streaks of light in the family.

TEN

The tie-breaking baseball game was scheduled for right after lunch on Friday. The game would decide the winning team for Spirit Week, and who would be treated to a pizza party.

When they got to school that morning, Zach asked Ms. Moriarty if Mr. Parker, the custodian, was back from his nephew's graduation yet. Zach was worried their team might not have its best chance to win without Mr. Parker coaching it.

"Mr. Parker called Mr. Haggerty about an hour ago," she said. Mr. Haggerty was the school principal. "He said he was about to get on the road, so he should be here before the game starts."

By the time they got down to the field, though, Mr. Parker still hadn't shown up. Now Zach was really worried they've have no one to coach their team.

Then he felt a tap on his shoulder.

"Just in time!" Mr. Parker said to Zach.

"I was starting to worry," Zach said, sounding relieved. "Our team is going to need all the help it can get to win this game."

"I'm the one who needs help today," Mr. Parker said. "Been one of those days where I can't seem to keep anything straight."

"No way," Zach said. "You're the most organized person in the whole school." He grinned. "Well, next to my sister."

"Not today," he said, shaking his head. "But

I did bring you something!" his voice sounded more cheerful now.

He reached into his bag and pulled out a box with a brand-new baseball inside.

"Like it? I thought it would be fun to have a new game ball." Mr. Parker said.

"Like it?" Zach said. "I love it."

Zach was so excited about the ball, he forgot to ask Mr. Parker why he didn't feel as organized as he usually did.

But he was about to find out.

Zoe was, too.

Zach played second base for the Blue team, and Zoe played second base for the White team. The game was scheduled to last six innings.

By the fourth inning, the White team was ahead 8–7. Brian Koppelman and Katie Madden had switched off pitching for the Blue team during the first four innings. Mateo was scheduled to come in and pitch the last two. Lily Holmes and Sam Carns did the same for the White team, and Alex Rather took over as pitcher in the bottom of the fifth inning.

The score remained 8–7 until the top of the sixth inning. The Blue team already had two outs when Zach came up to bat. Alex pitched him the ball and Zach hit it as hard and as far as he could over Lily's head in left field. As soon as Zach saw Lily chasing after the ball, he knew it was going to be a home run. He went flying

around second base, then third. His teammates cheered him on as he crossed home plate, tying the game.

By the time the next Blue team member was up to bat, Lily still hadn't retrieved the ball. It had not only gone past her, but rolled all the way down the hill behind the field.

When she finally came back up the hill, she called out to the others. "We're going to need a new game ball!" she shouted. "This one's all covered in mud!" Lily made a face as she gripped the dirty ball between her fingers.

Lily then tossed the muddy ball in to Zoe at second base. But instead of throwing it in to Mr. Parker, Zoe stared down at the ball in her hand.

"Time-out!" Zoe called, and came running in from the field, even though the Blue team was still batting.

"What's going on?" Zach asked, as Zoe ran up to where he was standing by the Blue team's dugout. "You want to give me my home run ball as a souvenir?"

"Nope," Zoe said. "I want to give you your Will Hanley ball."

"You sound pretty sure of yourself," Zach said.

"This time I am," Zoe said.

ELEVEN

The next minute, Zoe ran over to Mr. Parker and asked if he'd mind opening the equipment shed.

"Not at all. But we'll have to use the spare key. Good thing Ms. Moriarty knew there was one under the mat. Otherwise you kids would be out of luck."

"What do you mean?" Zoe asked.

"I lost my key to the shed. The one I always carry around on my keychain," Mr. Parker said, jingling the keys on his belt. "I can't imagine where it could have gone."

Zoe reached into her pocket.

"You mean this key?" she asked, holding it up.

He looked down at her, his eyes wide with surprise. "Where did you find that?"

Zoe told him all about finding the key outside the window of their classroom.

"I knew I must have lost it somewhere. I was rushing around so much the day I had to leave for my nephew's graduation," Mr. Parker said. "I just didn't know where I'd lost it. It must have fallen off my chain without me noticing."

They liked to joke that they could usually hear Mr. Parker coming before they saw him because of all the keys on his chain. There were so many, Zoe could see how he could have easily dropped one without knowing it.

"So, that's why you weren't feeling organized," Zach said. "You didn't have your key!"

"That's right," Mr. Parker said. "I felt lost without it. But I was in such a rush to get on the road."

"But did you happen to find a brand-new signed Major League ball before you left?" Zoe asked.

"I did pick up a ball right before I left," he said. "But I didn't see a Major League logo on it."

Zoe held up the ball Zach had just hit, the one covered in mud.

"Because maybe it looked like this," she said.

She handed Mr. Parker his key. He turned it in the lock and opened the shed. One more time, Zoe emptied the bag of old balls onto the ground.

The difference was, this time she knew what she was looking for. She quickly sat down on the grass outside the shed, and Zach sat next to her. Zoe knew they had to take more time going through the balls than the first time they tried.

One by one, they cleaned the dirt off the balls from the bag.

Not one was the Will Hanley ball.

Finally, there were only two balls left. Zach turned one over, looking at it from all angles. Then he sadly shook his head.

One ball left.

It had dirt caked all over it. Zoe banged it slightly on the shed door to chip the dirt off. Then she rubbed it on the front of her T-shirt.

That's when she saw the "WH" peeking out from underneath the mud. When she turned the ball around in her hand, she spotted the "Major League Baseball" logo.

She handed the ball to Zach.

"Here's your souvenir ball, big brother," she said, as she puffed out her chest with pride.

Behind them, they suddenly heard a huge cheer. Zach and Zoe turned and saw all their classmates crowding around them near the shed. They were happy Zach finally had his

Will Hanley ball back. And in that moment, it was as if they weren't the Blue team and the White team.

Just one third-grade team And they were all in it together.

But now it was time to finish the game and settle the championship of Spirit Week once and for all.

TWELVE

Everyone made their way back to the field.

"Now that I think about it, it must have been Sundance who knocked the ball off the windowsill," Ms. Moriarty said. "The wind blew the papers off my desk when I opened the window. I bent over to pick them up off the floor. He must have done it then. When I wasn't looking."

"I didn't know for sure how it fell out the window," Zoe said. "But yesterday, when I saw

Sundance push that ball of yarn off your desk, I was positive it was him."

"That's why you said 'thanks' to Sundance," Zach said. "For giving you another clue."

Zoe nodded. "When I saw the ball of yarn go over the side of the desk, I could just picture your ball going out the window. Made perfect sense."

"And the ball must have fallen in the mud because of the rain the day before," said Zach.

"That's right!" Zoe exclaimed.

"If I had put two and two together," Ms. Moriarty said, "I might have figured out sooner where the missing baseball had gone."

"That's okay, Ms. Moriarty," Zoe said. "Then there wouldn't have been a mystery to solve!"

"And in case you couldn't tell, Zoe loves a good mystery," Zach said.

"You know what I would love right now?" Ms. Moriarty said to Zoe. "Watching you find a way to win the game the way you just found your brother's ball."

"Sounds like a plan," Zoe said.

The White team had two outs in the bottom of the sixth and final inning. Zoe came up to bat with the bases loaded and the score still tied 8–8. Mateo was pitching for the Blue team.

Zoe thought, *If I can get a hit and win the game for my team, this will be an even more perfect day than it already is.*

Kari stood on third base, ready to run home. All Zoe had to do was hit the ball far enough for Kari to make the run and win the game. Mateo threw her a pitch right down the middle. Zoe hit the ball way over Mateo's head, past Zach, and into centerfield. Zach ran after the ball, but it was too late. Kari was already nearing home plate.

Zoe ran toward first base as she watched Kari sprint home for the winning run. The

game was over, with a final score of White team 9; Blue team 8.

Zoe's teammates crowded around her at first base and even chanted her name. When they were finished, she saw Zach standing in front of her, a smile on his face as big as the whole field.

He put up his left hand. Zoe put up her right. Then they spun and bumped hips and elbows, and finally gave each other high fives.

"On to the next game," Zach said.

"Or the next mystery," Zoe corrected.

"How about both?" her brother said. It was a day when sports had made another memory for both of them.

"Deal."

JOIN THE TEAM.
SOLVE THE CASE!

Help Zach and Zoe
get to the bottom of another mystery!

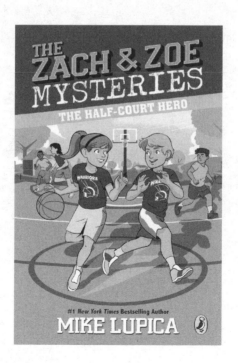

READY FOR ANOTHER MYSTERY?

LOOK FOR:

THE ZACH & ZOE MYSTERIES

THE FOOTBALL FIASCO